# Once upon a Munch there was a cow

# Munch!

### And OH! she did love to munch!

Written by Sarah Adams ~ Artwork by James Fletcher

AuthorHouse™
1663 Liberty Drive
Bloomington, IN 47403
www.authorhouse.com
Phone: 833-262-8899

This book is printed on acid-free paper.

ISBN: 978-1-6655-8773-0 (sc)
ISBN: 978-1-6655-8774-7 (e)

Print information available on the last page.

Published by AuthorHouse 10/18/2021

**author**HOUSE®

This book belongs to

..........................................

How many of our countryside friends
can you spot throughout Munch?!

She **munched** when the sun was high in the sky and when the rain was pouring down.

She **munched** when the birds woke up in the mornings, and when the stars came out at night.

She even **munched** when all the other cows lay down to sleep.

1

Munch was so busy **munching** one day that she didn't notice the farmer open the gate

into the next field.

She didn't hear the gate **creak** or the **soft thud** of the cows' hooves as they walked through, step by step, and far away from Munch.

Bertie Bunny was on the way back to his burrow when he saw Munch all alone, munching.

'Hello Munch,' Bertie said. 'What are you doing?'

'Munching,' said Munch. (Though she was hard to understand, with a mouthful of grass! )

'But why are you on your own? 'asked Bertie.

'I'm not,' replied Munch. ' Am I.....?'

And slowly she lifted her big black and white head, and slowly she looked around with her soft dark eyes. And slowly, very slowly,

Munch stopped munching.

'Oh dear' said Munch.

'Where are all the others?'

Shyly she looked at Bertie. 'Have you seen them?'

'No' said Bertie.

I could help you find them, if you like?...'

Bertie looked up at the sky, his gentle nose twitching.

'But I have to be back in my burrow before it starts raining.'

His little nose twitched even faster, and he hopped about anxiously.

'Come on Munch!'

Munch was not used to hurrying. She took one long sniff of the delicious grass and started to follow Bertie.

He was getting more and more worried.

There were big grey clouds in the sky, and a damp feeling in the air.

' I think they went this way Munch! ' called Bertie. ' Look! The grass is all squashed where the cows have walked! '

6

Munch was alone again. She'd never worried about that before.

She hadn't really made friends with the other cows. She'd always been too busy MUNCHING

Now Munch thought it might be nice to have a friend to walk across the field with. Her broad back was very wet, and cold drips slid down her legs.

Munch sighed a big sad sigh.

' Hello Munch '.
Susie Snail slipped
through the squashed
grass & stopped
in front of
Munch's nose.

' Don't you like the rain?
It makes slithering
SO much easier! '.

Munch shook her
big black and white
head, and blinked
her sad dark eyes.

' Look, ' said Susie.
'There are lots of us snails come out
to play. ' Munch stared at the other
snails, happily gliding through the grass.

' But I'm all alone, ' said Munch quietly.
' The other cows have gone.
Have YOU seen them? '

' No, 'Susie replied. ' I could help
you find them, if you like?
But I don't slither very fast.....'

' That's alright, '
said Munch.

' I don't walk
very fast! '

And slowly, very slowly, slower than grass growing or the leaves turning brown in autumn, Munch the big black and white cow and Susie the small brown and white snail went across the wet field together.

Susie slithered as fast as she could, but after half an hour they still hadn't gone very far.

Munch couldn't see any other cows. And she was getting very hungry....

'I'm sorry Susie, 'said Munch.
' I think I'll have
to carry on
by myself .'

Thank you for helping me.
' That's alright, ' puffed Susie.

' I'm all out of slither anyway!
Goodbye Munch! Good luck!' '

Munch carried on, carefully following the trail of squashed grass.

She didn't see the other cows watching her from the next field.

She didn't see the gate getting closer and closer until....

BUMP!

'Poor Munch,' said a kind voice. 'We wondered where you were.'

Munch lifted her sore head and looked into some big soft brown eyes, just like hers.

'Who are you?' asked Munch, quietly.

'I'm Mandy,' said the other cow. And here's

MISTY    MOSS    Moonshine

Marie                      MOXY

and

Moo

We missed you.

Munch felt a funny warm feeling spread up from her tummy. She stepped gladly into the next field.

Now Munch is friends with all the other cows. She still loves to **munch**.

But she loves to look at the blue sky on sunny days, and feel the cool rain on her back on wet days.

She loves to see the sparkling stars at night, and hear the birds singing when they wake.

And when the other cows lay down for a rest, Munch lays down with them.

Well, sometimes..!

# Have fun colouring in Munch and her friends!

With special thanks to:

To my friends
and family, who
believed in me.

To my very
patient publishers,
Authorhouse.

And most of all,
to my artist and
friend James,
who brought Munch
so delightfully
to life!

Lightning Source UK Ltd.
Milton Keynes UK
UKHW050629111121
393768UK00002B/88